# SEBASTIAN
## (Super Sleuth)
## and the
## Secret of the
## Skewered Skier

MARY BLOUNT CHRISTIAN

# SEBASTIAN
## [Super Sleuth]
## and the
## Secret of the
## Skewered Skier

**ILLUSTRATED BY LISA McCUE**

MACMILLAN PUBLISHING COMPANY
New York
COLLIER MACMILLAN PUBLISHERS
London

Macmillan Publishing Company
866 Third Avenue, New York, N.Y. 10022
Collier Macmillan Canada, Inc.
Printed in the United States of America
10   9   8   7   6   5   4   3   2   1

Library of Congress Cataloging in Publication Data
Christian, Mary Blount.
Sebastian (super sleuth) and the secret of the
skewered skier.
(Sebastian, super sleuth)
Summary: While on a ski trip to the Frozen Dreams
resort, Sebastian, dog detective, and his master John
run into a case of jewel theft.
[1. Mystery and detective stories. 2. Dogs—Fiction]
I. McCue, Lisa, ill.   II. Title.   III. Series: Christian,
Mary Blount.   Sebastian, super sleuth.
PZ7.C4528Sf   1984      [Fic]      83-19569
ISBN 0-02-718450-1

To Mary Helen Chapman

# Contents

# 1
# Jogging John's Memory

Sebastian's keen ears detected footsteps outside the door, and he was immediately alert. It was his day off—his and John's—but a detective is always ready, twenty-four hours a day, seven days a week.

He yawned, trying to shake the sleep from his head. *Rrrrrr-rupft!* he barked. Sebastian (Super Sleuth), the greatest four-legged detective anywhere, was on the job.

*Tha-wack!* The mail slot in the door clanged shut as envelopes fluttered to the throw rug beside the hairy hawkshaw. Only the mail carrier. It's a good thing! Sebastian thought smugly. An intruder wouldn't stand a chance against this clever canine.

He gave a final *Rrrrrr-rupft* before sniffing at the envelopes. Maybe one of them had coupons for a free hamburger, a pizza, or even a steak dinner for two.

A scuffling sound behind him diverted his attention. John—John Quincy Jones, the other half of the detective team—came into the room, his Adidas squeaking against the hardwood floor. He was wearing his warm-up suit. Sebastian groaned. That meant John was going jogging. And he'd probably expect Sebastian to go jogging with him, running around in circles in the park, getting nowhere but exhausted.

"Was that the mail I heard?" John asked, giving Sebastian a friendly scratch behind the ear.

Sebastian's foot thumped. *Ummmmm.*

John gathered the mail and sat on the couch to sort through it.

Good, Sebastian thought. Maybe John'd forget about jogging.

"Umm," John said, as he went through the mail, "Mother's in the Bahamas again. Must be nice, huh, old man? A light bill—will it ever go down? —and—here, what's this?"

Sebastian climbed onto the couch—*ooft*—and settled down, resting his chin on John's shoulder. Fortunately, he'd learned to read as a puppy, although no one, not even John, realized this. It was a skill that was useful in his self-appointed job, that of assisting his human, a detective with the city police department.

He, Sebastian (Super Sleuth), had solved many of John's cases with the aid of his sensitive clue-sniffing nose and his uncanny ability to disguise himself.

"Oh, my goodness! This is from that contest I entered—a jingle in twenty-five words or less, 'Why I Like Fruit Fizzies For Snacktime.' I don't believe this! It's wonderful! Oh, it's—it's fantastic!" John hugged Sebastian and tousled his fur. "I've won a skiing vacation at Frozen Dreams Resort!"

Sebastian curled his lip. *I've* won? Not *we've* won? *I've* won? After all, if he, Sebastian the gourmet, hadn't gotten carried away one day and eaten all those yucky-tasting Fruit Fizzies, would John have had the required five box tops? He wiggled the stump of his tail and pressed his cold nose to John's cheek, whimpering pleadingly.

"Wow!" John said. "Am I ever glad I started jogging. I'd hate to go skiing without being in good physical shape."

Sebastian sprang to the floor and jogged around the couch a couple of times, barking enthusiastically. If he showed John he had a fuzzy body like a well-oiled machine—*pant*—ready for any rigorous task—*pant*—maybe he could jog John's memory and—*whew!* All that running was tiring.

"I'll have to make arrangements to get off work,

of course. And I'll have to get someone in to water my plants, and—Sebastian, quit running around, I can't hear myself think—and of course, there's you. I'll have to get you a reservation, too."

Sebastian leaped up, giving John warm wet slurps on his cheek. He remembered! What a wonderful human being John was! Sebastian yipped excitedly. A vacation!

"I wonder what I did with that kennel's phone number," John muttered.

Sebastian stopped slurping John and curled his lip. Kennel? Kennel! But a kennel is for—for dogs! John couldn't do that to the old super sleuth! No way! He slumped his body in a hang-dog fashion and rested his chin on John's knee. He whimpered, then burst into a mournful howl. *Ooooooooo.*

"Now, you aren't going to be a baby about this, are you?" John asked, scratching behind Sebastian's ear.

Thump, thump. Sebastian couldn't stop his foot hitting the floor, but he refused to look John in the eye. John needn't think he could dismiss him with a mere scratch behind the ear! He dropped to the floor, rolled over on his back and, putting all four feet into the air, dead-dog style, he moaned pitifully.

"Oh, all right, you silly dog," John said, laughing good-naturedly. "I guess the plane fare won't be

any more than boarding you at a kennel for a week. And I'll feel better, anyway, knowing you aren't giving them a hard time." He pinched Sebastian's stomach. "I wonder if the Frozen Dreams Resort has any activities for dogs. You could use the exercise."

Couldn't John tell that was not real fat? Sebastian wondered. It was only a safety margin of energy stored away, in case he got sick, or was away from food too long. He let John's remark pass. He was too happy to be included in the vacation to object. He needed a vacation badly. After all, the strain of detective work had taken its toll on the hairy hawkshaw's magnificent brain and fantastic furry body. Let the truth be known: Sebastian (Super Sleuth) needed a rest.

He yawned contentedly, anticipating lying snug and warm before the fireplace in a posh resort, watching the gentle snowflakes float past the frosted window. No burglars, thieves, or kidnappers for a whole week.

# 2
# Paws for Pictures

The next day Sebastian went with John to Chief's office. He dreaded asking for time off. It would be difficult for Chief to give them a vacation. After all, he and John set the brilliant course for other detectives to follow. Without them, the city could be in a shambles within the week. How could CPD manage?

He sat on his haunches, hungrily eyeing Chief's lunch, which had been brought in on a tray. A club sandwich and French fries—not very gourmet, but filling. Sebastian smirked. Let Chief try to claim he's dieting this time! He edged closer as John made his plea.

"I realize this will leave you short handed, Chief, but I'd really appreciate having my vacation early. The prize is good for next week only and—"

Chief's bushy eyebrows shot up, like two caterpillars in a jump-off contest. He guffawed. "You're kidding! Short handed? Why, having you and that walking fleabag out of the city is like adding ten to the force!" He punctuated his insult with another hearty laugh.

John blushed. Sebastian emitted a low growl. The nerve of Chief! That—that—cat owner! Indignantly Sebastian sucked up the French fries, snapped up the club sandwich, and turned on his heels in disgust. Take that! he thought smugly.

"Get that food thief out of here," Chief yelled. With a flourish, he signed his name on the vacation permit and shoved it into John's hand. "At least I'll be able to eat in peace for a week!"

The worst part of any day was facing Chief. That behind them, John and Sebastian spent their lunch and coffee breaks shopping for rental skis and heavy wool gear for John.

John could save a lot of money and trouble, Sebastian figured, if only he'd grow fur.

Although it seemed the day to leave would never get there, it finally did. Sebastian trotted alongside John, who struggled with skis and luggage, toward the check-in counter at the airport. Sebastian was on his best behavior.

"I'd rather wait to board Sebastian until the last moment," John told the attendant checking the luggage and tickets. "This is his first flight."

Sebastian blushed right through the fuzz on his chin. He glanced around to see if anyone was listening. Must John tell the world that a dog of his vast experience and expertise had never flown? After all, he had watched *Dawn Patrol* and *Airport*. He'd memorized every procedure, just in case he ever had to bring a plane in. He'd imagined what it would be like, being a passenger, being served a hot meal on a tray, watching the clouds pass by—

"Come on, old fellow," John said. "It isn't time yet. Let's see what all those people over there are looking at."

Immediately Sebastian (Super Sleuth) spied the crowd of men and women with pencils and notebooks and with flash and video cameras. They were gathered at the gate from which Sebastian and John's plane was scheduled to leave.

Oh, dear, Sebastian thought. The media had found out that the greatest dog detective in the world—the universe—was going on vacation. They no doubt wanted pictures and a statement concerning the safety of the city during his absence. Well, John could handle the statements—he spoke their language. But nothing could substitute for the noble profile of the cunning canine, the hairy hawkshaw, for their pictures.

Sebastian worried only momentarily that having his picture made public might compromise his

undercover work in some future investigation. After all, criminals read the papers and watch television, too. He dismissed that.

Wasn't he a master of disguise? He'd been a gypsy dancer, a bearskin rug, a raccoon coat, a maitre d', and—the most difficult disguise in his career—that of an ordinary dog. Who'd ever recognize that fabulous face hidden behind a pirate's eye patch or an Arab burnoose?

Shrugging off the danger, Sebastian leaped into the center of the crowd and sat on a trunk next to a gaudily dressed woman. He broke into his most winsome, panting grin.

"Hey!" a man with a camera shouted. "Somebody get that dog out of the way! I can't get a good shot of Miss Diamonds!"

Sebastian blushed. No one had recognized him after all. So the old master disguiser had totally fooled this crowd of sensation-hungry reporters. At least news of his and John's leaving the city unprotected hadn't been discovered, he concluded, skulking to the edge of the crowd.

He eavesdropped and found out that the woman in the too-fancy dress and too much jewelry was Lotta Diamonds, a publicity-seeking movie starlet. She was going to a convention of jewelers.

"Dah-lings," she cooed, kissing her fingers and

pretending to throw kisses to the reporters. "I love you! Ummmm, kiss, kiss!" She turned, throwing kisses in every direction, and as she did the diamonds she wore around her neck, on her fingers and wrists, and in her ears flashed and sparkled in the glare of the flash cameras.

Publicity hound! Sebastian thought in disgust. How can she be such a show-off? Feeling a tug at his collar, he looked up to see John.

"Come on, old fellow. Time for you to board the plane."

Sebastian trotted toward the gate.

"No, boy," John called. "You don't go that way. I hate to do this to you, old fellow, but I'm afraid no dogs are allowed in the tourist cabin."

No tourist cabin? Sebastian thought. That's quite all right. He preferred first class anyway.

A redcap stood nearby with a dolly. There was a large cage on the dolly. Surely John didn't mean—

"In you go, old man," John said. "You'll ride in the special cargo bay. Don't worry now. The part you're in isn't with luggage and stuff. You'll be where it's pressurized and you'll have plenty of air, so just relax and try to enjoy the flight."

Sebastian dug in his heels and spread his legs wider than the cage door. They wouldn't take him without a fight!

John and the redcap together shoved and jammed until they squeezed Sebastian through the door. As he was wheeled unceremoniously toward the loading dock, Sebastian glared at John. This is a fine way to treat a master detective—like a common, ordinary dog!

He might have to start out in the cargo bay, but he vowed not to stay there. Was not he, Sebastian (Super Sleuth), a master, not only of disguise, but also of escape? His computerlike mind immediately sorted through his options.

# 3
# To Greater Heights

Sebastian glowered at the attendants who shoved his traveling cage into the live-cargo bay. They obviously didn't know with whom they were dealing. He, Sebastian (Super Sleuth), was not ordinary cargo! Immediately he set to work, jimmying the latch on the cage. Nothing could hold this hairy Houdini!

At last the door gave way and he tumbled into the open bay. Maybe there was still time to get out, find a suitable disguise, and enter the passenger cabin. He scratched at the door, whimpering. Too late. His stomach churned, and the trembling beneath his feet told him the plane had taken off. He'd have to find another exit.

The cunning canine remembered a late, late movie he'd once seen. The pilot had moved freely from one bay to another. There must be another way out.

Yes! His keen eyes spotted the door. It must lead to the hold where the meals are stowed, directly below the passenger-level kitchen area. If his memory served him correctly—and it always did—there should be a small elevator for the flight attendants between the two areas. Perhaps he could slip up that way and join the other passengers, taking a seat, preferably by a window.

He squeezed through the small door and found himself, as he'd expected, in the food storage area. And he saw something else—something that would aid him in his plan. A flight attendant's outfit—styled like a Swiss Alpine costume with its own matching kerchief—was on a hanger by the door. The name tag said *Nan*.

Quickly Sebastian wiggled into the uniform. He stepped into the elevator, which was just big enough for an attendant and a serving cart, and pushed the *up* button with his nose. It shot up with sickening speed, leaving his stomach below, it seemed.

"There you are! You must be Nan," a woman in a similar outfit exclaimed as he stepped from the elevator. "Welcome to Skylyte Airways. We thought you'd missed the flight. My name's Heidi."

Sebastian, startled, whimpered slightly.

"Oh, my!" Heidi said. "You do have a terrible case of laryngitis. Well, you don't have to talk much. Just see that everyone's comfortable and fed. Take this tray to 4A. And watch out for him. He's the worst grouch we've ever had! And do be careful of your footing. It's getting a little bumpy, but it always does when we start serving food, doesn't it?"

Sebastian nodded his understanding, sighing wearily. He dared not blow his cover. They were liable to send him back to the cargo bay and that terrible, humiliating cage. He snatched the tray in his teeth and made his way down the aisle toward 4A. Goodness, but the food smelled delicious! Beef burgundy over buttered noodles, hot rolls, and chocolate mousse for dessert.

"It must really be getting bumpy if you're on all fours, huh, gorgeous?" the man on the aisle in row

10 said. He chucked Sebastian under the chin.

Thump, thump! His foot reacted. Sebastian hurried past before a low growl could escape his fuzzy lips.

The man in 4A had his wrist chained to a briefcase in his lap. And the stewardess was right. He was a grouch!

"What'd you do—come by slow boat? This stuff's cold! And what's that on my dessert—coconut or dog hair? Skylyte must've raided the garbage cans for this junk!" The Grouch took the tray without so much as a thank you.

Sebastian, through heroic effort, kept his cool. He offered the man a panting smile.

"This stewardess looks like a real dog," he mumbled to the passenger sitting in 4B. "Little airlines get all the rejects."

Sebastian resisted the urge to nip him on the ankle, but lingered momentarily, eavesdropping. He wondered what the man did for a living that required a chained briefcase. He'd ruled out diplomat—The Grouch didn't have the tact for that job. But what could he be?

"The jewelers' convention started this morning. My boss wasn't going to let me attend at all—afraid I'd have too good a time since it's at a skiing resort, I guess," he said, bitterness lacing his voice. "He makes me so mad sometimes I have to jump on my trampoline for an hour, just to get rid of the tension. Do you think that bothers him? No!" He patted the briefcase. "But he forgot a bunch of the jewelry he was going to display, so I get to deliver it. Big deal! If there was a return flight today I wouldn't even get to spend the night! Someday he'll be sorry for treating me like this." Sebastian saw a sinister sneer cross the jeweler's lips as if he already had a plan in mind.

The Grouch was talking about the same convention that publicity-happy actress was going to. No wonder the briefcase was chained to the man's wrist —there could be millions of dollars worth of jewels in there!

Sebastian made his way back down the aisle and snatched another tray. His nose quivered at its close proximity to the food. He could no longer stand the pain of hunger! Quickly he snapped up the beef burgundy, deftly leaving the noodles intact.

Guilt ridden, he took the tray to seat 5C and was surprised to see it was John. He was sitting next to that gaudily dressed actress.

John stared at the noodles. "No meat? If I didn't know positively that my dog was locked in a cage in the cargo bay I'd swear that he'd been into this!"

Sebastian kept his head turned away slightly. It

would be no T-bones for a week if John spotted him.

Lotta Diamonds was still draped in all that jewelry. Sebastian glared at her out of the corner of his eye. She'd probably sat next to John deliberately, the way she was fluttering her long lashes at him, smiling her glossy-lipped smile. *Humph!*

She tapped the necklace, shrugging. "Oh, dahling, of course I'm not nervous about wearing such expensive jewelry. It's part of my image. My public expects it."

"I thought actresses kept their real jewels locked in bank vaults and wore only imitations," John said. "Wouldn't that be much safer?"

"I have insurance—lots of it." She flashed her smile at him again.

Snarling, Sebastian went to get another tray. He should've dumped that one in her lap, he thought disgustedly. The way she was looking at John—the way John was looking at her! *Humph!*

Before he'd finished serving, Sebastian had eavesdropped on the man in seat 6B, who Heidi said was an ex-millionaire who'd lost all his money and his chain of health spas in the silver market, a gymnast who thought skiing would improve his coordination, and a group of other people who had won vacations just as he and John had.

When he was through he stood on his hind legs,

resting his front paws against the door, and peered out the porthole. All he could see were great fluffs of clouds. His stomach churned a bit and he was anxious to reach the ground.

A bell sounded and Heidi announced that passengers should fasten seat belts. Sebastian scrambled into the elevator and down to the hold, where he shimmied out of the flight attendant's dress, regretting the thin layer of fur he'd left on it.

He scooted through the door and slipped into the cage just as the wheels of the plane squealed on touchdown. Everything was going just fine. It'd been a rather enjoyable trip, despite the exhausting service he'd been required to perform to keep from being discovered.

Now he would get his reward—rest and relaxation from his grueling job keeping the city free of crime.

The cargo bay door opened, letting in bright light reflected from a blanket of snow. Sebastian wagged his stump of a tail vigorously, eager to romp and forget his job for a while.

Still, he couldn't rid himself of an uneasy feeling. A jewelers' convention, with all those precious gems, would be a terrible temptation to a thief.

# 4
# The Skewered Skier

A bus waited at the passenger exit. It said FROZEN DREAMS RESORT LIMOSENE. Some limousine, Sebastian thought. The driver helped load all the luggage.

"Watch out for those black leather suitcases," the grumpy jeweler demanded. "You're not going to let that—that animal ride in the limo with us, are you?"

The driver looked at Sebastian and shrugged. "If he's going to Frozen Dreams Resort, I am. It don't make me no difference."

The jeweler stomped on board, grumbling something about disgusting dogs.

Sebastian, nose in the air, trotted onto the bus. As he passed the jeweler he shook vigorously. A fine cloud of dog hair settled on the man's blue serge pants. Satisfied, Sebastian settled into a seat next to a window so he could see the scenery.

Lotta Diamonds sat next to John. The man who said he was a gymnast, the ex-millionaire, and some of the other free vacation winners came aboard, too.

Sebastian rested his chin on the sill and watched the scenery pass by his window. He could just see himself schussing and gliding effortlessly down the slalom of one of those snow-capped mountains— Sebastian, Super Skier!

The tire chains clinked rhythmically against the recently cleared road as the bus bounced and slid along the route to the resort.

Soon the bus came to the foot of a mountain whose peak was hidden in a layer of clouds. Keeping to the inside of a narrow road that had been carved from the rocky mountain, the bus wound its way upward. Cautiously Sebastian peered out the window. The bus seemed to be teetering on the edge of the world. His stomach did a quick flip-flop and he squeezed his eyes shut tight. His head reeled from the dizzying height.

At last they rounded a pile of jagged rocks to see a large cedar chalet with a cheery-looking snow-covered roof. It was as if they'd been transported to Switzerland. The bellhops, wearing traditional Alpine costumes, unloaded the luggage from the bus.

Sebastian walked under a sign that said "Welcome Jewelers—Special Appearance by Lotta Diamonds." Sebastian noted with satisfaction that there was no "Welcome, Sebastian (Super Sleuth)" sign. They were unaware they had the world's greatest dog detective among them—and his sidekick, of course. It would be so embarrassing—one's name on a marquee, the constant requests for paw prints, the insistent crowd of admirers!

By the time Sebastian and John had recovered John's luggage and gotten into the lobby, the grouchy jeweler—his name was Hobart Rotyn— was already bawling out the hotel clerk because his room wasn't close enough to the conference room.

"I'm sure it will be small and uncomfortable, too," he growled at the bellhop, brushing a swatch of dog hair from his pants. "And be careful with those bags, for goodness' sake. Why is the dining room closed? What kind of resort is this?" he muttered.

A thoroughly disagreeable fellow, Sebastian concluded. No wonder his boss didn't want him around any longer than necessary!

John got his room key and he and Sebastian rode the elevator up to their floor. In the room Sebastian reared up on the window sill and looked out. In the distance he could see skiers careening wildly down the mountainside. It was starting to snow. He wagged his tail appreciatively.

John came to stand by him. "It's beautiful, isn't it, old fellow? I can hardly wait to get onto the slopes, that is—ahem—after I meet Lotta in the lounge for a cup of Swiss chocolate." John blushed. "She thinks I'm interesting company, she said."

Sebastian curled his lip. Didn't that woman have other things to do? Like meet the jewelers who were paying for her trip? Why did she have to pick on John? Besides, Sebastian had never heard of Lotta Diamonds. If she was so famous, why hadn't he seen her on the "Late, Late Show" on television?

John unpacked his clothes and pulled Sebastian's bowl and a sack of dry dog food from his suitcase.

Surely John didn't expect him to eat that! Not when there were so many famous Swiss dishes available just for the asking! He'd handle his own meal planning, thank you. Sebastian leaped onto the bed, bouncing a moment. Not too bad, but where would John sleep?

He yawned. Sebastian realized he was still exhausted—dog tired, in fact. He decided to take a nap before exploring the resort.

When he awoke it was nearly dark. Yodeling and the tinkle of Swiss bells floated up from the lobby. Sebastian yawned and stretched. He blinked at the clock. Six-thirty. It must be that entertainment the little brochure mentioned. He rode the elevator down and stepped into the lobby. Four men in

Alpine costumes were singing and playing. Vacationers in their woolly ski togs lounged around the fireplace clinking their cups of wassail and singing with the group.

Sebastian's keen eyes scanned the crowd, locating familiar faces. He didn't see the grumpy jeweler. It was just as well—he seemed to spoil everything. John leaned against a wall near the fireplace, talking with a woman. The ex-millionaire was talking with Lotta Diamonds, who floated from group to group, chatting. Sebastian saw the gymnast in the middle of a group of attentive women. Crutches leaned against his plush burgundy chair. His leg was in a cast. One arm was in a sling.

"Oh, you poor dah-ling," Lotta Diamonds cooed. "Your first afternoon on the slopes and you've already had a nasty fall. How terrible!"

The gymnast, whose name was Rocky Ridges, moaned dramatically and nodded. "Actually it was my own fault. I skewered my foot with the pole and when I jumped from the pain I lost my footing and tried to go around both sides of a tree at the same time."

"Ooohhh," one of the women said. "I was out there all afternoon. I didn't see it happen. I'm so sorry you got hurt."

Sebastian couldn't help but wonder what kind of

gymnast Rocky Ridges was. Anyone so clumsy as to ruin his whole vacation must be pretty bad. He'd come up here to ski, and now all he could do was sit around with his foot propped up and let women wait on him. Poor guy, Sebastian thought.

The conference room where the jewelers' meetings were held was closed and locked. A sign at the door said, "No trespassing. No conventioneer will be admitted without a badge. This area is protected by burglar alarms."

With millions and millions of dollars in jewelry on display, Sebastian could understand why they weren't letting just anyone in there.

He settled by the fireplace, his sensitive ears tuned to the crackling of the hickory logs, his eyes blinking sleepily as he saw images in the leaping flames. This was the life. When he retired from crime prevention this was the sort of life he'd lead, Sebastian decided.

Just as he dozed off there was a terrible rumble, like a freight train. The entire chalet trembled. The yodelers fell silent. Sebastian sat up, alert and ready. What was that?

The lights flickered, then went out. The only light was from the fireplace. The crowd of vacationers muttered and stirred uneasily until the lights flickered on again.

The hotel manager came in and raised his hand reassuringly. "A snowslide knocked out the electricity for a moment, that's all. But our emergency generator kicked in, just as it's designed to do. No problem—at least nothing major."

"What do you mean, nothing *major?*" John asked.

The manager rushed to the desk phone and lifted the receiver. "Just as I thought. The lines are down. But don't worry. We have plenty of food and a good generator, and the snowplows will clear the road again—as soon as anyone realizes what's happened. Until then, those of you scheduled to leave tomorrow will be our guests a little longer, that's all. Heh, heh."

Sebastian remembered the grumpy jeweler. He gets to stay longer after all. His gain is our loss, Sebastian thought, wolfing down a piece of apple pie someone had so thoughtfully abandoned by the hearth. Being trapped is so hunger provoking!

A gray-haired man stepped forward. He was the president of the jewelers' conference. "I'd like to check the burglar alarm in the conference room. I don't want to take any chances that it was damaged."

"The electricity was off only for a moment. I see no prob—" The manager shrugged. "Very well. If you insist. Come with me."

Interested, Sebastian trotted along behind them. Maybe he could get a look at the alarm system, see what kind it was: laser beam, ultrasonic. He was just a curious canine cop on, or off, the job.

The manager opened the door. The three of them walked into the room and immediately the alarm sounded a raucous blare.

"See?" the manager said smugly. He pushed a series of buttons on a wall panel. The alarm stopped. "The windows are also wired, and anyone trying to open one would set off a second alarm. Neither alarm could have been off for more than a second, just long enough for our system to switch over to the generator. No problem."

The president's face was pale. "Then tell me, please, where are the jewels that belong in *that* case?"

Sebastian peered past them at the display cases. His spinal fur stood on end. One of the showcases was empty!

# 5
# Some Vacation!

As far as Sebastian could see, while the jewelry seemed undisturbed in other areas, the display case at the front of the room was completely empty. The doors stood open, the velvet cloth the gems had rested on was in disarray.

Abandoning all thought of a vacation, Sebastian (Super Sleuth) let his keen mind click into action.

"What are we going to do?" the manager asked, wringing his hands. "The roads are closed until the snowplows clear them. Our phones are out. What can we do?"

John came up. "Excuse me, what's going on?" he asked, looking from the manager to the jewelers' president and back again.

Ignoring him, the president turned on the manager. "I think you'd better do something! You told me this was a safe place. Get your hotel security person in here—right now."

The manager stuffed his hands into his pockets. "I can't. That is—we don't have one. I thought the alarm system would be enough of a guarantee."

"Don't have one!" the president said. "Don't be stupid! Every hotel has *somebody*! When we signed up for this conference here, you said—"

"We—we did—then. But the season has been so bad, we had to cut expenditures somewhere."

*Hmmm*, Sebastian thought, no wonder half the guests were winners of contests. The hotel people'd probably talked the Fruit Fizzies company into buying a large block of rooms and meals for the contest, figuring that would help them get through the season.

"I heard the alarm system go off. Did my dog—" John began. "Sebastian! There you are. Shame, boy, you—"

"It wasn't your dog that set it off, and please don't come any farther in here," the president said. "We'll have to keep this room clear until we can get through to the police."

"I'm a detective," John said, flashing his CPD badge. "Perhaps I can help."

Perhaps *we* can help, Sebastian corrected mentally. *We*—will John never learn?

"First, we should determine whether or not the jewels actually have been stolen," John continued.

"We must see if anyone took the jewels back to his or her room, or put them into the hotel safe."

The manager's shoulders sagged in relief. "Yes, of course. That is probably what happened."

By that time the entire crowd of jewelers and vacationers had gathered outside the conference room. It didn't take much time until John, with the help of the president, had determined that the jewels had indeed been left in the conference room —that they definitely had been stolen.

"I suggest that you reactivate the alarm system," John told the manager. "Post one of your hotel employees outside the door—just in case. All you people return to the lobby as you were," he told the curious crowd. "I'll want an inventory list of the missing jewels and I'll want to question each of you individually, beginning with Mr. Norburch, whose entire collection was taken.

"I naturally don't have any special detection equipment with me—I'm on vacation," John apologized to the manager. "But if you'll get me some cellophane tape and some flour from the kitchen I'll try to make do. If the cook will sift it three or four times for me, it should be fine enough."

So John was improvising a fingerprint kit. He could dust with the fine powder, then lift with the tape. Not ideal, but better than nothing. Sebastian wagged his tail eagerly. John was doing a grand job—almost as good as he, Sebastian (Super Sleuth), could do.

The hotel manager reactivated the alarms, locked the door, and posted a bellhop at the door as John had suggested. Then he hurried off to instruct the cook about the flour.

The cunning canine wandered among the hotel guests, eavesdropping and clearing abandoned plates of any leftover doughnuts and sandwiches. The people would pay little attention to a dog among them—they were blissfully unaware of greatness in their midst—so he could perhaps pick up clues that a human might not hear.

He found out that Mr. Norburch, the jeweler who'd lost his entire collection, was the boss of Hobart Rotyn, The Grouch—the same man, Sebastian remembered, who'd threatened that someday his boss "would be sorry." Had "someday" arrived? Perhaps The Grouch had stolen the jewels to get even. After all, there hadn't been any theft before he got to the hotel. And The Grouch had planned to leave on the morning plane, before the conference reopened its doors. He hadn't counted on the roads being closed, or anyone checking the conference room early. He seemed a prime suspect.

The gymnast hobbled up to John on his crutch.

"Would it be all right if I went to my room? I'm in terrible pain and—"

"Of course," John said, understandingly. "I'll save you to talk to until last—say an hour and a half from now. In fact, if the rest of you would like to go to your rooms, I'll do door-to-door interviews."

Quite a few of the guests took John up on his offer, including the ex-millionaire, Lotta Diamonds, The Grouch and his boss, who said he did have his jewels fully insured and wasn't too upset about the theft. He was afraid, though, that someone might copy his original designs and sell them.

Sebastian mentally added Mr. Norburch to his list of suspects. After all, he didn't stand to lose any money, and he'd gain a lot if he collected on the insurance *and* kept the diamonds, too. Besides, anybody who'd hire The Grouch couldn't be all good!

The covert canine heard a couple of women whispering about Lotta Diamonds. Unnoticed, he eased over near them and lay down, flattening himself against the floor. The bearskin rug disguise was an oldie, but a goodie. It worked every time. Undetected, Sebastian cocked one ear to eavesdrop.

"Do you think those diamonds are real? I doubt it, don't you? I mean, they're so—so big!"

The second woman nodded. "Well, I heard her

career was finished. She probably had to sell off her real diamonds—the fancy way they live, you know. She's probably hoping the publicity she'll get from being at the jewelers' convention will remind some director that she's available for movies."

The first woman raised one eyebrow knowingly. "She can always go back to the circus and ride an elephant or swing from a rope by her teeth, or whatever she did before she got discovered in Hollywood."

The two giggled wickedly, then lowered their voices. Sebastian found their gossip so tasteless—interesting, but tasteless.

But what if those gossips were right? What if Lotta Diamonds had sold her real diamonds and had only paste jewelry now? What if she planned to use the stolen jewelry to replace them?

Sebastian mentally added her—the flirt!—to his list.

His stomach rumbled. Detectives cannot live by doughnuts alone, Sebastian reminded himself. Besides, someone should check on the chef, make sure the thief hadn't slipped the stolen diamonds into tonight's blue plate special. He slipped into the kitchen and successfully devoured two platefuls of sauerbraten before the chef spotted him and threw him out. Huffily, the old hairy hawkshaw rejoined the guests in the lobby.

John questioned each guest on his or her whereabouts and took a list of jewels from each jeweler before checking the conference room for clues. "I'd like you to let me in now, but please lock the door behind me," he told the guard.

The bellhop admitted John and Sebastian scooted in behind him. Immediately, the raucous alarm sounded.

"Very good," John said. "It's working fine. Anyone walking in here would break the beam and set off the alarm immediately." He deactivated the floor alarm, but left the window alarm system on.

Sebastian wagged the stump of his tail eagerly.

He thought this case could be quickly solved. John would test the fingerprints. He'd find those of The Grouch and/or Mr. Norburch, or maybe Lotta Diamonds, then they could enjoy the rest of their vacation. But suddenly Sebastian froze in mid-wag.

More jewels were missing!

# 6
# A Sticky Situation

Close examination revealed that at least six more pieces of expensive jewelry had been stolen—with the alarm working and the guard posted just outside the door.

It was not only humiliating to the cunning canine detective to have the place burgled with him and John right there, it was also puzzling. How could anyone get in without setting off the alarm?

John had said, and Sebastian agreed, that anyone walking around the room or opening one of the windows would set off the alarm. The guard insisted that no one had entered or left the room and he had heard nothing—just a slight creak. But the floors settle in the cold, expanding and shrinking, and he thought nothing of the creak, he'd said.

John immediately began dusting for fingerprints. It was obvious from some of the smudges that someone wore gloves.

"But *all* the jewelers wear gloves when they are handling the gems," the president told John later when it was his turn to be questioned in the conference room. "They don't want the oils from their skin to mar the shine of the jewelry."

They weren't making this case any easier! Sebastian thought. Still, he, Sebastian (Super Sleuth)—and John, of course—would solve the mystery. They had to! He blushed, thinking of what Chief would say if they didn't!

"At least we know no one can leave until the roads are cleared," John said. "That gives us time to solve this—I hope."

He was probably thinking about Chief, too, Sebastian figured. Slowly the hairy hawkshaw sniffed his way around the room, looking for a clue—anything that would tell him how some thief could enter and leave with the jewelry without disturbing the window or floor alarms.

The floor alarm system would be triggered when someone walked across the room, breaking the beam. The other system was connected to the window latches, so opening any one of the windows would set off a loud noise, too.

Sebastian reared up on one of the window sills and sniffed. His keen nose led him to a small piece of adhesive tape. Could it have been deliberately, carefully placed across the latch to give a false signal? The alarm would sense the window was locked when it was actually open for entry from the outside.

John had disconnected the floor alarm while they were in there, but he'd left the window alarm connected. It should be easy enough to test. Sebastian grabbed the piece of tape between his teeth and pulled, growling. It came loose and the second alarm sounded noisily. John rushed to his side.

"What are you doing, Sebastian? Here now, what is this stuck to your tooth? Tape? But where—?"

John ran his finger over the latch. "It's sticky—just like the tape. I wonder—" He placed the tape over the outline of the stickiness and the alarm shut off. He pulled it off and the alarm sounded again. "Someone fixed this window so they could come through it without setting off the alarm."

Sebastian sat on his haunches, a smug panting grin on his face. Not bad, John, for a human, he thought.

"But how could they not set off the floor alarm?" John asked aloud.

Sebastian slumped to the floor, his chin resting on his paws. He hadn't thought of that. The only one who could do that sort of thing would be a magician—or— He jumped up, licking his whiskers. Or perhaps someone either leaped or swung from something—a chandelier? The guard *had* mentioned a creaky sound.

Yes, the chandeliers hung in convenient spots. The right person could make it from table to table without ever touching the floor. Someone in excellent physical shape. Rocky Ridges was a perfect suspect. Of course, Sebastian ruled out the gymnast immediately. With his arm in a sling and his leg in a cast, he could hardly swing from chandeliers.

Those gossips had said that Lotta Diamonds had been in the circus before she became a movie star. Maybe she was a trapeze artist. Of course, the ex-millionaire had owned a bunch of health spas, and had probably worked out constantly. So it wouldn't do to dismiss him as a suspect. And Hobart Rotyn said he worked off his anger on a trampoline. That takes a lot of physical dexterity, too.

John stood on the window sill, his hands on his hips. "If someone jumped from here—no, it'd take a kangaroo to jump from here to the first showcase. Hmmm. . . . Maybe they had a grappling hook on the chandelier—"

Sebastian sighed wearily. Clever, John. Slow, but clever.

John removed the tape so the window latch would really lock, then he reactivated the second alarm and knocked for the bellhop to let him and Sebastian out.

Lotta was at the registration desk. It was the first time Sebastian had seen her without diamonds draped all over her. She had a carved jewelry box with her and she was making a big fuss.

"I don't want to stay here another minute, trapped with some horrible thief! I feel so—so scared! At least, if I can't leave I want all my jewels locked in your vault right now. Right this minute!"

The assistant manager jumped up, his fingers clutching his baloney sandwich so hard he nearly tore it in half. "Yes, ma'am. Of course, ma'am. Just a minute, ma'am!" He nervously twirled the dials of the small vault.

"Hurry!" Lotta Diamonds snapped.

The poor assistant manager shoved the box— and his baloney sandwich—into the vault and slammed the door shut.

John explained his (and Sebastian's) theory to the manager and the conference president. Then he rounded up the suspects, those he thought had the agility to get past the floor alarm—the ex-millionaire, The Grouch, and Lotta Diamonds. Sebastian was grateful that John hadn't let a pretty face cloud his thinking about suspects!

"You certainly can't suspect me!" Lotta Diamonds

protested. "Besides, I have an alibi. I helped Rocky Ridges up to my room, poor dah-ling, and prepared him some hot tea and soup in my kitchenette. We talked until I heard about the second theft and decided to store my jewels."

That explained why Rocky Ridges didn't answer his door when John had gone up to question him.

The Grouch had been with his boss all along, making out an inventory report for the insurance company. And the ex-millionaire had returned to the lobby with several other people who vouched for him.

Either it was someone they didn't even suspect, or one of these three was lying, Sebastian cleverly concluded. The only ones who knew each other before today were The Grouch and his boss. None of the others would have any reason to protect each other, Sebastian figured.

Maybe the answer was outside the chalet, out where the thief had entered through the window. He decided to take a look outside.

The temperature was dropping. Sebastian sneaked back to their room and skittered into John's fleece-lined parka. Then he scooted around to the windows outside the conference room. Goodness, it was cold! He wished now he'd worn John's boots, too. He felt as if the pads of his paws might freeze

to the ground. Sebastian spotted a pair of skis resting against the wall. Knocking them to the ground, he shoved his paws into the straps. Ah, that was better, having the skis between his paws and the snow!

If only he could— Suddenly his keen eyes spotted a dark figure crouched in the shadows. He tried to respond, but it was too late. The figure wheeled on him and the hairy hawkshaw felt a thud against his head.

Cold wind tousled his fur and pellets of snow stung at his fuzzy cheeks. Sebastian was careening down the snowy slope! His skis were locked into a bob run carved by the many skiers that day— Sebastian the Schussboomer!

Recovering his wits and with expert *Vorlage*, he smoothly adjusted his center of gravity, gradually bringing the runaway skis under control, then to a quick stop.

Slowly, Sebastian sidestepped his way back up the slope toward the chalet.

His mind cleared by the chill, he ran through his clues as he climbed. Perhaps the dark figure in the snow was the thief. But what was he doing outside? And who was it? Had he mistaken the old super sleuth for John? After all, he was in John's parka.

Perhaps the thief believes that he and John already know his identity. And there is nothing more dangerous than a criminal who is one up on the crime stoppers!

# 7
# Surprise, Sebastian!

As he worked his way up the slope toward the chalet, Sebastian worried over the clues. Sometimes there weren't enough suspects. This time, there were too many. And the only one obviously capable of such athletic feats was unable to do those things because of his broken arm and leg.

But someone had shoved Sebastian—hard—outside the chalet.

There was Hobart Rotyn, the grouchy jeweler, who'd threatened to get even with his boss. He worked out on a trampoline. Or it could be his boss after all that insurance money. There was the ex-millionaire, who'd probably like a fresh start on his next million. And he'd owned spas, so he was fairly athletic.

There was the hotel manager, who needed the money to keep the resort going. There was Lotta

Diamonds, whose career was not exactly on the upswing. But then she had an alibi—she was with the gymnast at the time of the last theft. Sebastian sighed wearily.

He pushed through the revolving door, shook off John's parka and, teeth chattering, edged his way toward the fireplace. John was there, questioning the suspects. Sebastian found a plate of abandoned fritters and warmed his feet on them before finishing them off.

"This is ridiculous!" Hobart Rotyn complained. "I'm going to my room. I won't stand for any more questioning."

Calmly John explained to The Grouch that *he* was in charge right now, at least until the snowplows got through, and he wanted the man to stay right there.

Sebastian broke into a panting grin. It was just like one of those late, late movies. "Inspector Chan will see you in the drawing room at midnight."

He slumped to the hearth, carefully avoiding the leg cast of Rocky Ridges stretched out in front of him. Idly he traced the pattern of the adhesive tape around the cast as he listened to John and the suspects.

Suddenly the old hairy hawkshaw sat up, alert. Didn't doctors have to chisel away the cast once the patient no longer needed it? Wasn't a cast one solid

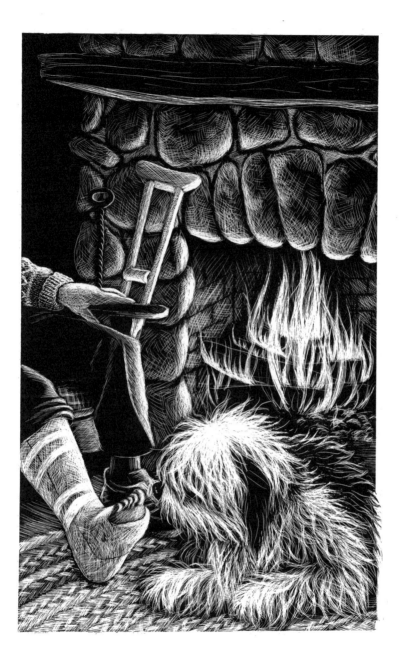

piece? Why did *this* cast need adhesive tape around it—the same kind of tape that had been on the window?

He leaned closer until his nose was right next to the cast. This cast had a fine line down the side of it, as if—as if—yes! He was sure now.

Growling, Sebastian tugged at the piece of adhesive tape that crisscrossed the line.

"Sebastian! Stop!" John yelled. "No, boy! What are you doing?"

Lotta Diamonds screamed and Rocky Ridges jumped to his feet just as the cast opened up and slid off his leg. It was a phony, just as he, Sebastian (Super Sleuth), had deduced!

Oh, cleverest of canines, how do you do it again and again? he thought smugly. He was a bit disappointed, though. He'd hoped against hope that the diamonds were hidden inside.

Rocky Ridges suddenly moaned and slumped back to the chair. "That dog! My leg—"

"Forget the act!" John said. "We all saw you standing on that leg, and it was perfectly sound. In fact, I'd bet the arm cast is a phony, too!"

Sebastian sat back on his haunches, pleased. He, himself, was just about to say that.

Now the pieces of the puzzle were fitting together. The gymnast was able to enter through the window and leap and swing on the chandeliers from table to table, never once disturbing the alarm beam. But when could he have fixed the window so it would open without setting off the alarm? Without a badge, Rocky Ridges was not allowed in that room. That meant he had to have had help.

Suddenly the old super sleuth remembered something important—the missing clue. If Rocky Ridges was the thief, then he couldn't have been with Lotta Diamonds. That means she lied. And if she lied, she was probably in on the theft. And *she* would've had the perfect opportunity to fix the window. As the honored guest of the conference, she could come and go in that room as she pleased.

While the ex-millionaire and The Grouch guarded the gymnast, John and the hotel manager searched his room. And because John had—finally!—made the connection between Rocky Ridges and Lotta Diamonds, they searched her room, too. In fact, to Sebastian's surprise, she welcomed their search.

She must've been sure the jewels weren't there or she would have protested. Then it hit him. Of course the jewels weren't in the room. Hadn't Lotta Diamonds insisted loudly that the hotel put her diamonds into the vault? That had to be where the stolen gems were.

Sebastian raced around the registration desk to

the vault, growling and tugging at the handle. Maybe he could make John understand.

John caught on pretty fast—after all he'd worked with the master detective now for four years; he'd have learned a lot in that time.

"Sebastian! Now what are you doing?" he shouted. "Here I am trying to conduct an investigation and you—of course! Open the vault," he told the manager.

Lotta Diamonds turned pale. "That's my personal jewelry box, and I forbid you to open it!"

"Then we'll wait for a search warrant," John said. "Until that time, the box remains in the vault."

Sebastian figured that could be late the next day. He decided to help John out. He saw there was no lock on the box, so he leaped up, barking wildly, and "accidentally" knocked the box from John's hand as he was returning it to the safe. It tumbled to the rug and burst open. And there were the stolen jewels—all of them.

Now Sebastian understood what had happened outside earlier. Lotta had substituted the stolen gems for her own fake diamonds in the jewelry box. But she had to hide her own somewhere. Rocky Ridges had buried them in the snow, probably figuring that by the time the snow thawed and the phony jewels were discovered, it'd be too late. He and Lotta Diamonds would be out of the country and safe. But they hadn't counted on the old super sleuth's seeing Rocky Ridges burying the phony jewels.

The one thing Sebastian hadn't figured out was that Lotta Diamonds and Rocky Ridges were secretly married. They had both performed in the circus until she got a chance in the movies. The two thieves were clever, but not so clever as to fool this cleverest of canines!

The jewelers were extremely pleased to get their gems back and continued their conference. The snowplows made it through the next day and Mr. Norburch sent The Grouch back home, which made the resort a lot more pleasant for everyone.

John took Lotta Diamonds and Rocky Ridges to the sheriff in town. The rest of the vacation turned out to be pretty nice, except for those flirty women hanging around John, telling him what a great detective he was.

As usual, John accepted all the credit for solving the case. He even said that Sebastian probably wanted the vault open because he smelled the missing baloney sandwich that the nervous clerk had accidentally locked away with the jewels. Sebastian's nose was somewhat out of joint about that!

Still, it had turned out to be a grand vacation: just enough mystery to make it exciting, but a lot of relaxation, too.

By the end of the week, Sebastian was ready to go home, though—even if it meant seeing Chief again. The old super sleuth missed the action!

Instead of going to the airport, however, the limo took them to the train depot. Sebastian wagged his tail eagerly. He hadn't been on a train since he was a mere puppy!

"I decided to take the train this time," John told the ticket clerk. "That airline was less than ideal, I'll tell you. Would you believe I found fur in my chocolate mousse?"

While John bought his rail ticket and made arrangements for a traveling cage, the old super sleuth made other plans. He padded off in search of a proper disguise, something that would get him out of that dreary baggage area and into the thick of things.

A conductor's unifom? he pondered. A brakeman's? It was so difficult to continually top one's own brilliant disguises. Suddenly, he spotted the perfect disguise!

Sebastian shimmied into the train engineer's overalls and bandanna. He wiggled enthusiastically as he anticipated the thrill of the throttle beneath his paw!

He checked to see that John was nowhere in sight —it'd be dry dog food for a week if his human caught him! When all was clear he dashed eagerly toward the diesel's shiny cab.

He suddenly remembered this movie on the "Late, Late Show" about a great train robbery and broke into a panting grin.

Let them come. He, Sebastian (Super Sleuth), was ready!

MARY BLOUNT CHRISTIAN has written many popular books for children, including *April Fool; The Devil Take You, Barnabas Beane!;* the "Goosehill Gang Mysteries," and three previous books about Sebastian: *Sebastian (Super Sleuth) and the Hair of the Dog Mystery, Sebastian (Super Sleuth) and the Crummy Yummies Caper,* and *Sebastian (Super Sleuth) and the Bone to Pick Mystery.* Her *The Lucky Man,* a Ready-to-Read Book, was named a "Best Book of the Year 1979" by *School Library Journal.* Ms. Christian is also the creator and moderator of the syndicated PBS-TV series "Children's Bookshelf" and teaches college writing courses in Houston, Texas, her home.

LISA MCCUE is a talented young illustrator of children's books. A graduate of Southeastern Massachusetts University and Hartford Art School at the University of Hartford, Ms. McCue lives in Tappan, New York.